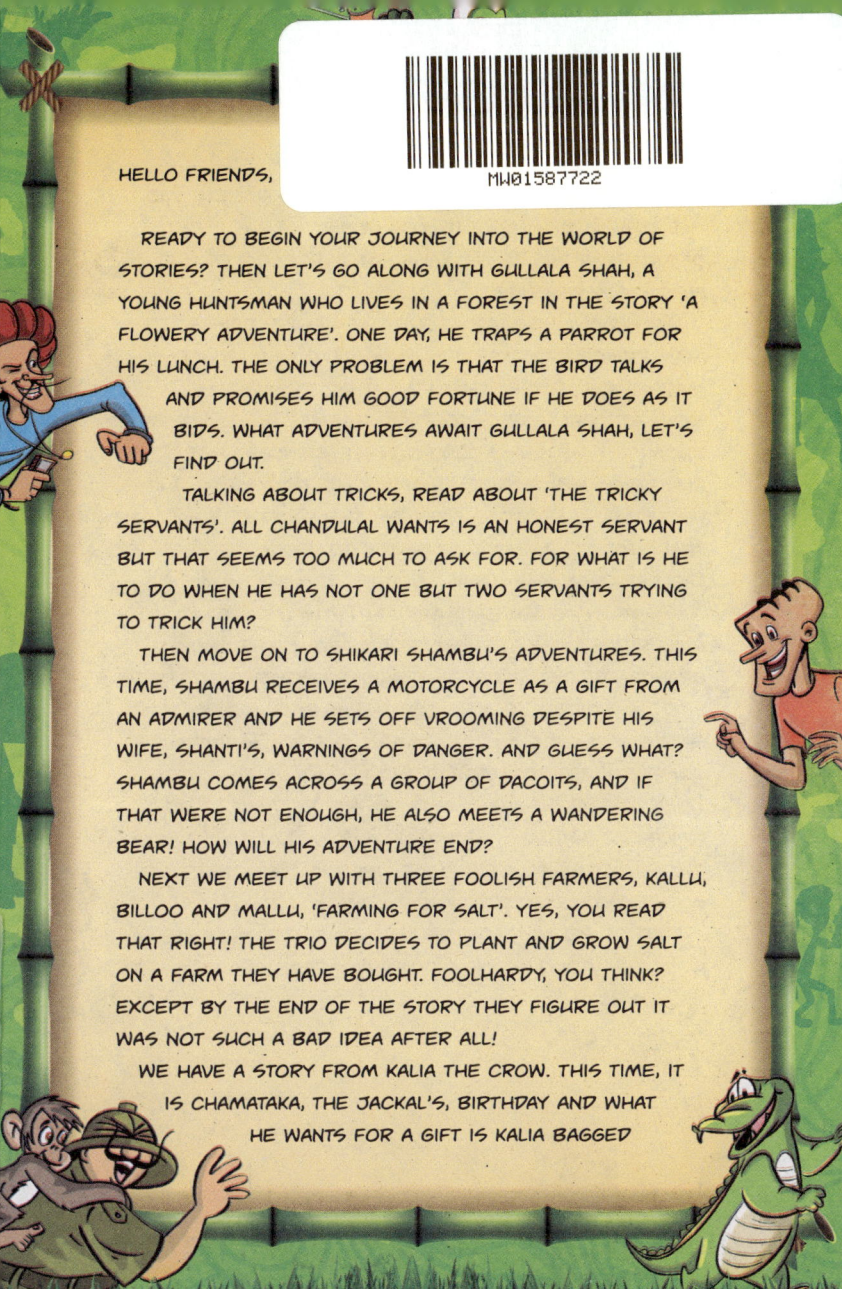

HELLO FRIENDS,

READY TO BEGIN YOUR JOURNEY INTO THE WORLD OF STORIES? THEN LET'S GO ALONG WITH GULLALA SHAH, A YOUNG HUNTSMAN WHO LIVES IN A FOREST IN THE STORY 'A FLOWERY ADVENTURE'. ONE DAY, HE TRAPS A PARROT FOR HIS LUNCH. THE ONLY PROBLEM IS THAT THE BIRD TALKS AND PROMISES HIM GOOD FORTUNE IF HE DOES AS IT BIDS. WHAT ADVENTURES AWAIT GULLALA SHAH, LET'S FIND OUT.

TALKING ABOUT TRICKS, READ ABOUT 'THE TRICKY SERVANTS'. ALL CHANDULAL WANTS IS AN HONEST SERVANT BUT THAT SEEMS TOO MUCH TO ASK FOR. FOR WHAT IS HE TO DO WHEN HE HAS NOT ONE BUT TWO SERVANTS TRYING TO TRICK HIM?

THEN MOVE ON TO SHIKARI SHAMBU'S ADVENTURES. THIS TIME, SHAMBU RECEIVES A MOTORCYCLE AS A GIFT FROM AN ADMIRER AND HE SETS OFF VROOMING DESPITE HIS WIFE, SHANTI'S, WARNINGS OF DANGER. AND GUESS WHAT? SHAMBU COMES ACROSS A GROUP OF DACOITS, AND IF THAT WERE NOT ENOUGH, HE ALSO MEETS A WANDERING BEAR! HOW WILL HIS ADVENTURE END?

NEXT WE MEET UP WITH THREE FOOLISH FARMERS, KALLU, BILLOO AND MALLU, 'FARMING FOR SALT'. YES, YOU READ THAT RIGHT! THE TRIO DECIDES TO PLANT AND GROW SALT ON A FARM THEY HAVE BOUGHT. FOOLHARDY, YOU THINK? EXCEPT BY THE END OF THE STORY THEY FIGURE OUT IT WAS NOT SUCH A BAD IDEA AFTER ALL!

WE HAVE A STORY FROM KALIA THE CROW. THIS TIME, IT IS CHAMATAKA, THE JACKAL'S, BIRTHDAY AND WHAT HE WANTS FOR A GIFT IS KALIA BAGGED

AND TAGGED. CHAMATAKA MANAGES TO NET KALIA BUT WILL THE CLEVER CROW TAKE IT LYING DOWN? HE HAS PLENTY OF TRICKS UP HIS WINGS. KALIA NOT ONLY ESCAPES BUT ALSO PLOTS REVENGE!

MOVING ON, WE READ ABOUT 'THE WEAVER PRINCE'. NOW, PRINCE RATNAKAR IS SUPPOSED TO WED PRINCESS MADHUMALA, EXCEPT THAT HIS FATHER, THE KING, IS WORRIED THAT HIS SON DISPLAYS NO SKILL. HE IS WORRIED BECAUSE THAT IS THE CONDITION THE PRINCESS HAS PLACED ON HER FUTURE HUSBAND. SHE THINKS THAT A KING SHOULD ALSO LEARN TO EARN A LIVING! FIND OUT WHAT TRADE PRINCE RATNAKAR MANAGES TO LEARN AND WHETHER THE PRINCESS MADHUMALA AGREES TO MARRY HIM.

GUESS WHAT? WE HAVE A STORY FROM BELOVED CHILDREN'S AUTHOR, RUSKIN BOND, ABOUT 'THE DAY GRANDPA TICKLED A TIGER'! GRANDPA BOND TAKES A GROUP INTO THE FOREST LOOKING FOR TIGERS EXCEPT THEY DON'T FIND ANY DESPITE A LONG DAY. BUT THE TRIP IS NOT A COMPLETE WIPE OUT, FOR GRANDPA BOND FINDS A LOST TIGER CUB. HE NAMES IT TIMOTHY AND REARS IT AT HOME. TIMOTHY EVENTUALLY GROWS UP AND IS SENT TO THE ZOO BUT GRANDPA HAS A SURPRISE WHEN HE VISITS THE TIGER IN THE ZOO. READ ON TO KNOW MORE!

STORIES DELIGHT. STORIES ALSO MAKE ONE THINK. WE HOPE THIS BOUQUET OF STORIES AND FEATURES HELPS YOU DO BOTH.

HAPPY READING,
RAJANI THINDIATH
EDITOR-IN-CHIEF, *TINKLE*

Make Your Own Plasticine

You will need:

An empty bowl, 1½ cups flour (maida), 1 cup salt, 2 tablespoons cooking oil and a few drops of food colouring.

Method

1. Mix the salt, flour and oil into the bowl.
2. Add the water and food colouring slowly.
3. Knead into a smooth dough.
4. Now you can make different shapes with the plasticine.
5. When you have finished playing reknead the plasticine into a ball, put it into a plastic bag and refrigerate. Add a few drops of oil if it gets too dry.

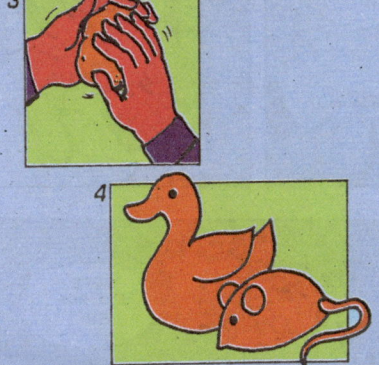

Sent by : Neville Mehta

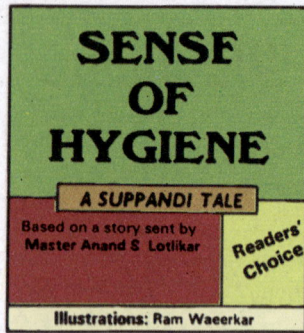

THE MACHINE PAR EXCELLENCE!

FACT FANTASY
Anant Pai • Pradeep Sathe

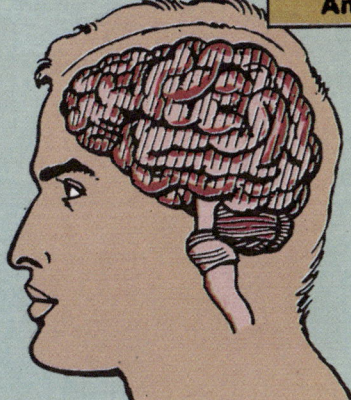

THE WRINKLED GREY COVERING OF THE BRAIN IS MADE UP OF 9,000,000,000 CELLS!

IF ALL THE BLOOD VESSELS IN THE HUMAN BODY WERE LAID END TO END, THEY WOULD STRETCH MORE THAN 15,000 KILOMETRES!

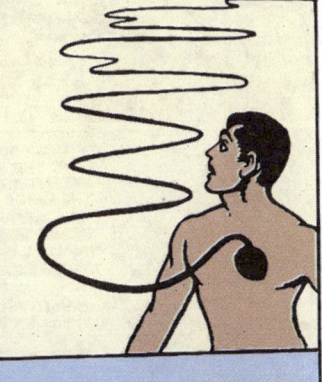

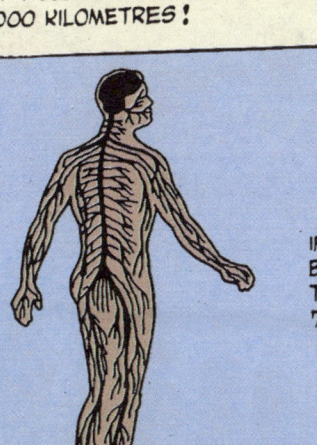

IF ALL THE NERVES IN THE HUMAN BODY WERE LAID END TO END, THEY WOULD STRETCH ABOUT 75 KILOMETRES!

It Happened to me...

It was summer. A neighbour of mine, Mr Karan Patnaik had three mango trees in his garden. One afternoon, I got into his garden. I plucked some mangoes. Unfortunately, Mr Karan was at home. He saw me plucking the mangoes. I jumped over the wall and ran away. That very evening he came to our house. He handed me a bag and said, "Take it, boy." By that time my heart was thumping. My face turned pale and sweat poured out. My father and Mr Karan had a long talk. Then he left our house. I was relieved that he had not complained about me. As soon as he had left our house, I went to the kitchen to see what was in the bag. To my surprise, there were mangoes in it. I felt very repentant and the next day I went to his house and apologised. He said, "Never mind, boy, children always do that." Drops of tears fell on my cheeks. I vowed never to steal again.

This true-life incident sent by: Ritesh Ku. Panigrahi

THE BEAR HUG

This happened 30 years ago. Our grandfather was a highly adventurous person who thought nothing of camping alone in the thick forests of the Nilgiris. One day he and a friend of his went camping to a forest called "Annae Katti". They were hacking their way through thick undergrowth when grandfather felt a heavy hand on his shoulder. He thought it was his friend. All of a sudden he saw two bear cubs in front of him. He turned to tell his friend about it—and got the shock of his life. The big hand was a big bear's paw. Thinking quickly, he pulled out his gun and fired into the air. The bear startled by the noise fled. Grandfather had missed a warm BEAR-HUG!

A true-life incident sent by Sameer Nanjapa & Yashika Ganapathy

PRECAUTION

Illustrations: Gautam Sen

Readers' Choice

Based on a story sent by: Hercules Rebello

THE SUPERWOMEN OF SPORTS

Script: Shobha Rao
Illustrations: Ramanand Bhagat

When the Olympic games were first held in ancient Greece, women were neither allowed to participate nor to watch the games. Breaking this rule meant the death penalty.

It is said that once a mother of a boxer, determined to watch her son fighting, entered the stadium in disguise. When her son won, she leapt into the arena and was discovered. However the judges showed mercy to her for her courage and for the fact that her father and brothers were all Olympic champions.

WHEN THE MODERN OLYMPICS WERE REVIVED IN 1896, WOMEN WERE ALLOWED TO WATCH BUT STILL NOT ALLOWED TO PARTICIPATE.

WOMEN WERE FIRST ALLOWED TO TAKE PART IN THE OLYMPICS ONLY IN 1928 AT AMSTERDAM. JUST FIVE EVENTS WERE OPEN TO THEM THEN. THESE WERE ALL FIELD AND TRACK EVENTS.

LONG DISTANCE RUNNING WAS CONSIDERED BEYOND THE PHYSICAL CAPABILITY OF WOMEN TILL 1984. IN THAT YEAR, JOAN BENOIT OF THE UNITED STATES WON THE FIRST WOMEN'S MARATHON IN LOS ANGELES.

THE 10,000 M RACE INTRODUCED FOR THE FIRST TIME IN 1988 AT SEOUL WAS WON BY OLGA BONDARENKO OF THE SOVIET UNION.

JOAN BENOIT SAMUELSON OF THE UNITED STATES.

OLGA BONDARENKO

It Happened To Me

CREAM MIX-UP

My face-cream had got over, so I took some from my mother's bottle, applied it and then went to school. I found my classmates staring at me in a strange way.

After school, when I went home and looked into the mirror, I got the shock of my life. The skin of my face was peeling off. Alarmed, I went running to my mother. She laughed and told me that she had replaced the cream in the cream-bottle with glue. So it was not my skin, but dried glue which was peeling off my face.

Based on a true-life incident sent by:
Md Arshad Patel

WRONG THIEF

During the Navratri festival, my father had allowed me, for the first time, to take part in the garba provided I came home by 12 o'clock. Feeling very excited I agreed, but while leaving I forgot to tell my father that I was taking the house key with me.

When I got back from the garba, it was about two o'clock. Realising that I was late, I decided to use my key to enter the house. When my father saw the door opening from outside, he thought it was a thief who had broken the lock. He immediately cornered me, covered me with a blanket and started shouting, "Thief, thief!" Before long the entire neighbourhood was awake and present. When they removed the blanket and discovered me there was a great deal of amusement.

Based on a true-life incident sent by: **Dhiraj Garg**

MISSED FLIGHT

I used to love making paper rockets during mathematics lectures. On one such occasion, when I was in my eighth standard, in spite of my good aim the paper rocket zoomed off and lodged itself in my teacher's hair. She was unaware of it and the whole class burst out laughing at the odd sight.

Soon the teacher realised the addition to her hairstyle and being a nice teacher joined in the laughter. I had a tough time explaining what went wrong with my rocket. Since then I have stopped making paper rockets in class.

Based on a true-life incident sent by:
M. Maria Anitha

IMITATE AND LEARN

FACT FANTASY
ANANT PAI · SUHAS TAKLE

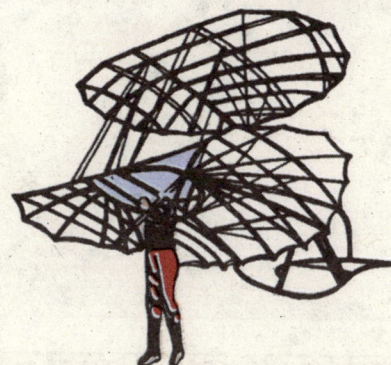

IN HIS EARLY EXPERIMENTS OF FLYING, MAN IMITATED THE BIRD. THE PICTURE GIVEN ALONGSIDE IS THAT OF LILIENTHAL'S FLYING MACHINE.

CARL BENZ INVENTED ONE OF THE FIRST SUCCESSFUL MOTOR CARS. IT RESEMBLED A TRICYCLE.

RAILWAY PASSENGER CARRIAGES OF THE 19TH CENTURY IMITATED THE DESIGN OF HORSE COACHES.

AN ENEMY BY INSTINCT

Script: Adil Rangoonwalla
Illustrations: Gautam Son

The ancient Egyptians looked upon it as sacred and called it the Pharaoh's cat.

But this long-bodied, short-legged animal is certainly not a cat. It is a mongoose!

The animal consumes a variety of food, including insects, centipedes, scorpions, rats, frogs, lizards and snakes. It is fond of eggs too.

MONGOOSE BREAKING AN EGG AGAINST A WALL

Mongooses are generally associated with snake fights. When a snake and a mongoose start fighting it is generally a fight to the finish. The mongoose erects its long hair and fights fiercely. Its agility and the long hair make it difficult for the snake to sink its fangs into the animal's body.

THE SNAKE BEING A COLD-BLOODED CREATURE TIRES FASTER THAN THE WARM-BLOODED MAMMAL AND THEN THE MONGOOSE MOVES IN FOR THE KILL.

THE HOSTILITY OF THE MONGOOSE AND THE SNAKE IS INSTINCTIVE! THERE HAS BEEN A CASE OF A MONGOOSE BEING REARED IN CONTROLLED CONDITIONS WHERE IT WAS NEVER EXPOSED TO A SNAKE. YET WHEN A RUBBER SNAKE WAS PUT IN FRONT OF THE CREATURE IT ATTACKED IT WITH ALL ITS MIGHT AND TRIED TO KILL IT.

THERE ARE SIX SPECIES OF MONGOOSE FOUND IN INDIA. THE LARGEST ARE THE STRIPE-NECKED MONGOOSE AND THE CRAB-EATING MONGOOSE.

SMALL INDIAN MONGOOSE

COMMON MONGOOSE

STRIPE-NECKED MONGOOSE

CRAB-EATING MONGOOSE

IN THE LAST CENTURY, THE MONGOOSE WAS TAKEN TO HAWAII, FIJI, AND THE WEST INDIES TO RID THESE PLACES OF RATS AND SNAKES. IT DID THE JOB ADMIRABLY AND THEN STARTED TO FEED ON GROUND-NESTING BIRDS AND POULTRY AND THUS BECAME A GREATER PEST THAN THE PESTS IT HAD GOT RID OF! SHOWN BELOW ARE SOME OF THE BIRDS ENDANGERED BY THE MONGOOSE.

HAWAIIAN DUCK

ST. LUCIA WREN

PUERTO RICO WHIPPOORWILL

ST LUCIA FOREST THRUSH

DESPITE ITS FEROCITY THE MONGOOSE IS EASILY TAMED.

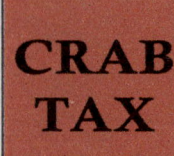

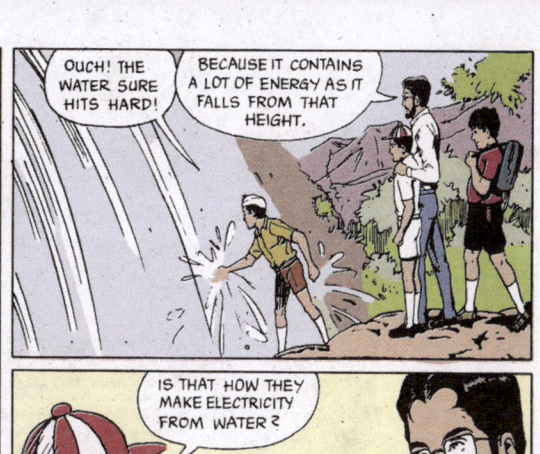

FACT FANTASY

Anant Pai • Pradeep Sathe

JUST MISCONCEPTIONS!

HOUSE SPARROWS

CHEEP CHEEP

Contrary to what poets believe, birds do not sing because they feel happy. Their song is in fact a challenge to other birds not to enter the territory, they have reserved!

Bees do not collect honey. What they gather is the nectar from flowers, which is converted in their body to honey!

Owls prey on mice, rats etc. only at night — not because they cannot see during the day, but because mice, rats etc. are active only at night!

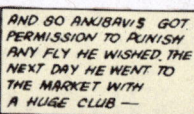

TANTRI THE MANTRI

Readers' Choice
Based on a story sent by Master Mahesh S. Newalker
Illustrations: Anand Mande

* BULLS REACT TO MOVEMENT, NOT COLOUR. TANTRI AND HOOJA DON'T KNOW THAT.

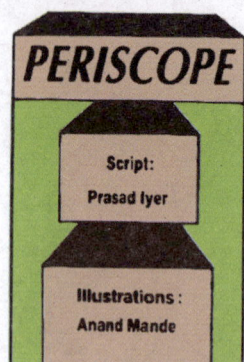

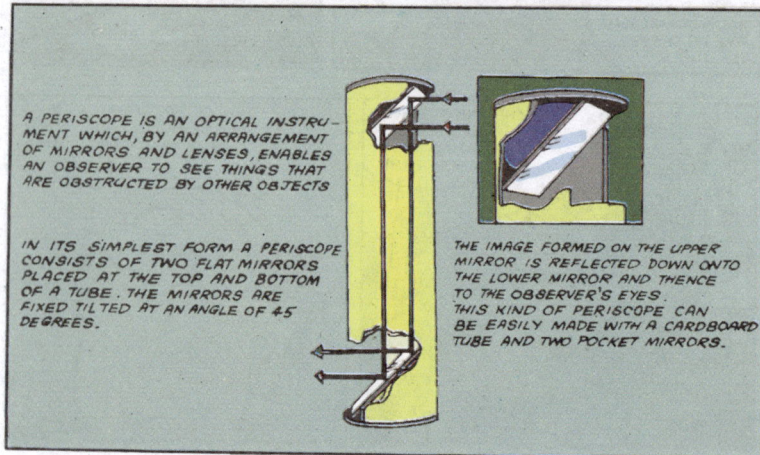

PERISCOPES HAVE MANY MILITARY APPLICATIONS.

A SOLDIER USING A PERISCOPE TO LOOK OUT OF A TRENCH WITHOUT EXPOSING HIMSELF TO ENEMY FIRE

BATTLE TANKS FITTED OUT WITH PERISCOPES ENABLE THE COMMANDERS OF THE TANKS TO OBSERVE ENEMY POSITIONS WITHOUT COMING OUT OF THE TANK

ALL SUBMARINES ARE FITTED OUT WITH PERISCOPES. THE TUBE OF THE PERISCOPE IS VERY LONG (12 METRES OR MORE) TO ENABLE THE VESSEL TO KEEP WELL BELOW THE SURFACE OF THE WATER.

BUT THIS PERISCOPE IS VERY COMPLEX. IT HAS SEVERAL LENSES TO MAGNIFY THE IMAGE.

IT ALSO HAS AN INSTRUMENT ATTACHED CALLED THE RANGE-FINDER WHICH ENABLES THE OBSERVER (USUALLY THE COMMANDER OF THE SUBMARINE) TO ESTIMATE THE DISTANCE OF THE ENEMY SHIP FROM THE SUBMARINE.

ONCE THE COMMANDER HAS SELECTED THE TARGET AND ESTIMATED ITS DISTANCE FROM HIS OWN CRAFT, HE GIVES THE ORDER TO LAUNCH THE TORPEDOES.

THE TORPEDOES STREAK OUT FROM THE SUBMARINES...

...AND EXPLODE AGAINST THE SIDE OF THE ENEMY VESSEL MAKING A HUGE GAPING HOLE

SOON THE STRICKEN SHIP SINKS AND THE SUBMARINE DIVES INTO THE SEA AND SLIPS AWAY.

THUS IN PEACE OR WAR, THE PERISCOPE IS A DEVICE THAT ILLUSTRATES HOW THE PROPERTY OF LIGHT REFLECTION CAN BE PUT TO USE.

WHY THE ANTARCTIC IS BEING EXPLORED

Anant Pai • Pradeep Sathe

THE ANTARCTIC CONTINENT, MORE THAN FOUR TIMES AS LARGE AS INDIA, WAS CONSIDERED A WASTELAND COVERED WITH A VERY THICK ICE CAP. ICEBERGS COME INTO BEING WHEN ITS GIANT ICE FIELDS ARE BROKEN BY OCEAN CURRENTS AND CARRIED AWAY INTO OCEANS!

THESE DREADED ICEBERGS CAN MEET WATER REQUIREMENTS OF NATIONS, IN THE YEARS TO COME, IF TOWED AWAY. A LARGE ICEBERG IF TOWED TO KANDLA IN KUTCH WOULD BE ENOUGH TO MEET THE WATER REQUIREMENTS OF THE DRY KUTCH AND EVEN RAJASTHAN FOR MANY, MANY YEARS!

ANTARCTICA HAS MORE COAL THAN IN THE REST OF THE WORLD! IT IS RICH EVEN IN MINERALS LIKE IRON ORE, COPPER, NICKEL, LEAD, MANGANESE, CHROMIUM, TIN AND EVEN URANIAM AND THORIUM. BUT FIRST MAN MUST FIND ECONOMICAL WAYS OF BORING THROUGH ITS ICE-LAYER (2 KM. TO 4 KM. THICK) AND THE ROCK UNDERNEATH.

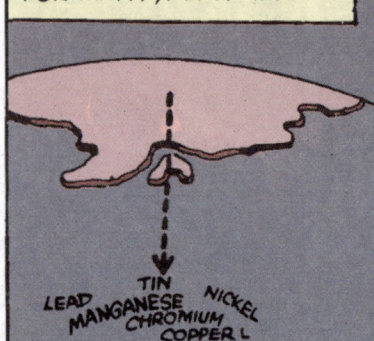

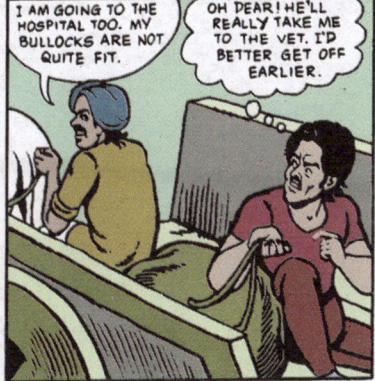

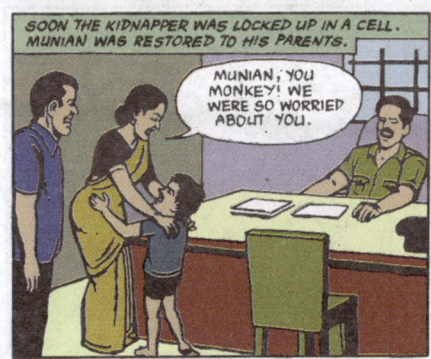

BEAKS, BEAKS AND MORE BEAKS

Script: Prasad Iyer
Illustrations: Gautam Sen

THIS PLUMP PIGEON IS WINGING ITS WAY HOME UNAWARE OF THE LURKING DANGER..

SUDDENLY, SWIFT AS AN ARROW, AN EAGLE SWOOPS DOWN AND GRABS THE PIGEON IN ITS TALONS.

THE CRUEL TALONS SPELL DEATH FOR THE PIGEON.

SOON THE EAGLE IS BUSY DEVOURING THE PIGEON. THE EAGLE HAS A SHARP, HOOKED BEAK IDEALLY SUITED TO TEAR FLESH FROM ITS PREY.

ALMOST ALL BIRDS OF PREY HAVE SHARP, HOOKED BEAKS, SINCE THE FLESH OF ANIMALS IS THEIR MAIN DIET.

SNOWY OWL

GOLDEN EAGLE

THE SHAPE OF A BIRD'S BEAK IS A CLUE TO ITS PRINCIPAL DIET AND SO WE SEE THAT EVEN SCAVENGING BIRDS, SUCH AS VULTURES OFTEN HAVE HOOKED BEAKS.

PURPLE HERON

SOME BIRDS LIKE THE HERON HAVE LONG DAGGER-LIKE BEAKS WHICH HELP THEM TO CATCH THEIR STAPLE FOOD, FISH.

SOCIABLE VULTURE

EGYPTIAN VULTURE

COMMON KINGFISHER

SIGNALS IN THE WILD

Script : Adil Rangoonwalla
Illustrations : Gautam Sen

SCIENTISTS HAVE ALWAYS BEEN FASCINATED BY THE SIGNALS USED BY SOME ANIMALS TO COMMUNICATE WITH EACH OTHER.
SIGNALS SERVE DIVERSE PURPOSES. THE MALE FIREFLY FLYING THROUGH THE INKY DARKNESS, FLASHING HIS LIGHT ON AND OFF, SUDDENLY SEES AN ANSWERING FLASH ON THE GROUND. IT IS A FEMALE SIGNALLING HER PRESENCE TO HIM.

WHEN A BEE DANCES ON THE HIVE, IT IS SIGNALLING THAT IT HAS FOUND FOOD. THE DANCE CONVEYS INFORMATION ABOUT THE FIND

A MINNOW THAT IS CAUGHT OR WOUNDED BY A PREDATOR RELEASES A CERTAIN CHEMICAL INTO THE WATER. OTHER MINNOWS DETECT THE CHEMICAL AND AT ONCE BECOME ALERT.

"RUN! THERE'S DANGER APPROACHING!" SAYS THIS PRONGHORN TO ITS FRIENDS. BUT IT GIVES THE WARNING SILENTLY — BY ERECTING THE WHITE HAIR ON ITS RUMP. THE SIGNAL CAN BE SEEN OVER A CONSIDERABLE DISTANCE.

AN AMERICAN SCIENTIST WAS STUDYING THE MACAQUE MONKEYS OF JAPAN. THESE MONKEYS MOVE ABOUT IN GROUPS. THE SCIENTIST NOTICED THAT OCCASIONALLY A MALE MONKEY WOULD CLIMB A TREE AND SHAKE IT SO VIGOROUSLY THAT THE LEAVES AT THE TOP OF THE TREE WOULD FALL OFF.

WHEN THIS HAPPENED, THE PARTICULAR GROUP OF MACAQUE MONKEYS THAT WAS FEEDING ON THE GROUND, QUIETLY LEFT THE PLACE. ON THEIR DEPARTURE, THE GROUP TO WHICH THE TREE-SHAKING MACAQUE BELONGED WOULD ENTER THE AREA AND START FEEDING.

IF AFTER SOME TIME A MONKEY FROM A THIRD GROUP CAME AND SHOOK THE TREE THE MONKEYS OF THE SECOND GROUP, IN TURN, WOULD QUIETLY LEAVE THE PLACE.

THE SCIENTIST REALISED THAT SHAKING A TREE WAS A SIGNAL DEVISED BY THE MONKEYS TO ENABLE THEM TO KEEP OUT OF EACH OTHERS' WAY AND THUS TO AVOID FIGHTS BETWEEN THE VARIOUS GROUPS.

ANOTHER INVESTIGATOR OF ANIMAL BEHAVIOUR DISCOVERED THAT THERE WAS A PECULIAR RUMBLING SOUND COMING FROM THE STOMACHS OF ELEPHANTS THAT WERE FEEDING AWAY FROM THE HERD.

IF A PARTICULAR ELEPHANT STOPPED MAKING THE RUMBLING SOUND, THE OTHER ELEPHANTS IN THE VICINITY WOULD AT ONCE GO TO SEE WHY IT HAD STOPPED SENDING THE SIGNAL. IN THIS WAY AN ELEPHANT IN TROUBLE COULD SUMMON HELP WITHOUT MAKING A SOUND, LITERALLY.

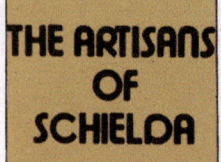

MISTAKES THAT PROVED BENEFICIAL

FACT FANTASY
Anant Pai • Pradeep Sathe

A WORKER OF A PAPERMILL IN BIRKSHIRE, ENGLAND, FORGOT TO USE THE SIZING MATERIAL ON ONE LOT OF PAPER, MANUFACTURED IN THE MILL. THE MILLOWNER THOUGHT OF USING THE PAPER AS SCRAP, BUT WHILE WRITING ON A SHEET OF THE "SPOILED" PAPER, REALISED ITS ABILITY TO ABSORB INK! THAT WAS HOW BLOTTING PAPER WAS "DISCOVERED"!

DR. ALEXANDER FLEMING

A HELPER OF DOCTOR ALEXANDER FLEMING FORGOT TO COVER ONE OF THE DISHES IN WHICH STAPHYLOCOCCUS GERM WAS BEING GROWN TO SEE ITS EFFECT ON SEA PLANTS. IN THAT DISH A MOULD HAD GROWN, WHICH SEEMED TO PREVENT THE GROWTH OF THE STAPHYLOCOCCUS GERM. PENICILLIN WAS DISCOVERED!

CHARLES GOODYEAR

ORDINARY RUBBER CRACKS DUE TO COLD AND MELTS DUE TO HEAT. ONE DAY GOODYEAR DROPPED RUBBER, CONTAINING A LITTLE SULPHUR, ACCIDENTALLY ON THE STOVE. IT DID NOT MELT, BUT TURNED HARD. THAT WAS HOW VULCANISED RUBBER WAS DISCOVERED, FROM WHICH TYRES, SHOES, ETC. ARE MADE.

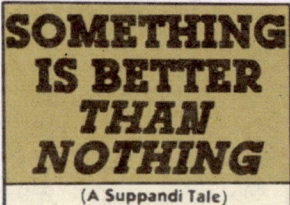

IT HAPPENED TO ME....

A true-life incident sent by C. Rahul, Bangalore

A true-life incident sent by Kalidas Narayan, Margao

When I was studying at a boarding school, just a day before the inspection of my room by the warden, I had accidentally broken a window pane. I had not reported it.

The next day, when the warden came, I was afraid that I would get a scolding. Instead he hurriedly inspected the room and saw the window without glass and told me to keep all the other window glasses as clean as that one. Till now I cannot forget this amusing experience.

Last year during the summer vacations we went for a holiday to Madras. One day on the terrace, my cousins, friends and I were playing the game, 'train train'. The game is played by holding on to the shirt or dress of the person in front of you. After some time my cousins and my friends were called downstairs by their parents and I was left alone. Suddenly I realised that someone was still holding my shirt from behind. I turned round to see who it was. To my horror, I found that it was a monkey. Without getting panicky I continued to play the game. This continued for about five minutes and then there was a loud thud downstairs. Hearing the noise, the monkey let go of my shirt and fled.

KALIA THE CROW

Script and Illustrations Prasad Iyer

Make Your Own Owl

You will need:
Wrapping paper of different colours. An empty tube – such as the one in which badminton shuttlecocks are sold.
Black fibre-tip pen, scissors and glue.

1.
Fold a piece of coloured paper in half. Trace or copy this figure on it.
Cut out the shape with the scissors and draw a pair of eyes on it. This is the head of the owl.

2.
Now cover the tube with coloured paper and glue it on.

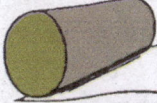

3.
Cut out the wings and the feet as shown, and stick them onto the tube.

4.
The owl is ready to decorate your showcase.

FINGERPRINTS

FACT FANTASY
Anant Pai • Pradeep Sathe

AFTER 30 YEARS

FINGERPRINTS ARE SPECIFIC TO AN INDIVIDUAL AND REMAIN UNCHANGED THROUGHOUT HIS LIFE! IN THE UNITED STATES FINGERPRINTS ARE TAKEN NOT ONLY OF CRIMINALS, BUT MEMBERS OF THE ARMED FORCES AND MANY CIVILIAN EMPLOYEES ALSO.

THE CHINESE USED FINGERPRINTS FOR IDENTIFICATION AS EARLY AS IN 700 A.D.

THE JAPANESE EMPERORS SMEARED BLOOD ON THEIR FINGERS AND PALM AND THIS PALM-PRINT SIGNATURE WAS A THING THAT LASTED AS LONG AS THE PAPER DID!

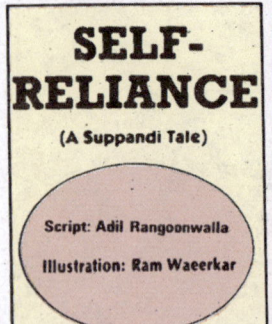

THE WORLD'S FAVOURITE DISH
• Script: Luis Fernandes • Illustrations: Gautam Sen

IT IS SAID THAT SOUP WAS FIRST MADE IN EGYPT IN THE DAYS OF THE PHARAOHS. THE STORY GOES THAT A SLAVE NAMED MENES STOLE A CHICKEN FROM THE PHARAOH'S KITCHEN AND BOILED IT.

BUT HE WAS CAUGHT BEFORE HE COULD EAT IT.

HE WAS BROUGHT BEFORE THE PHARAOH. THE PHARAOH WAS HUNGRY AND THE AROMA FROM THE POT WHICH MENES HAD BROUGHT ALONG WITH HIM, MADE HIM DROOL.

HE TASTED THE WATER IN WHICH THE CHICKEN HAD BEEN BOILED. THEN HE DRANK A SPOONFUL OF IT, THEN ANOTHER... AND ANOTHER ...TILL FINALLY HE HAD FINISHED THE BROTH. WHEN HE HAD FINISHED HE WANTED MORE. MENES WAS PARDONED AND APPOINTED A COOK IN THE ROYAL KITCHEN.

WHETHER THE STORY IS TRUE OR NOT, ONE THING IS CERTAIN: SOUP WHETHER MADE OF MEAT OR VEGETABLES HAS ALWAYS BEEN APPRECIATED BY RICH AND POOR ALIKE. SOUPS ARE HIGHLY NUTRITIOUS. A SURVEY OF 60,000 PEOPLE IN THE UNITED STATES ESTABLISHED THAT REGULAR SOUP EATERS ENJOY BETTER HEALTH THAN OTHERS!

"YES, I EAT SOUP EVERY DAY."

THE PEOPLE OF THE MEDITERRANEAN REGION BELIEVE THAT GARLIC SOUP PREVENTS MANY DISEASES...

...IN JAPAN, SEAWEED SOUP IS GIVEN TO WOMEN WHO HAVE JUST GIVEN BIRTH...

...AND IN KOREA, PEOPLE BELIEVE THAT SNAKE-MEAT SOUP CURES NEURALGIA*, BUILDS UP STAMINA AND HELPS ONE LIVE LONGER.

PERHAPS THE MOST UNUSUAL MATERIAL OUT OF WHICH SOUP IS MADE IS BIRDS' NESTS. BIRDS' NEST SOUP IS A TRADITIONAL CHINESE DISH. IT IS MADE OUT OF THE SMALL NESTS OF A PARTICULAR SPECIES OF SWIFT. THESE BIRDS NEST IN LARGE COLONIES IN CAVES. THEY STICK THE NESTS ONTO THE WALLS OF THE CAVES WITH SALIVA. THE NESTS TOO ARE MADE LARGELY OF SALIVA. SOME NESTS ARE MADE ENTIRELY OF SALIVA AND THESE ARE THE ONES WHICH ARE MOST PRIZED FOR MAKING BIRDS' NEST SOUP.

MEN CLIMB UP ON POLES AND KNOCK THE NESTS DOWN.

* DISEASE CHARACTERISED BY SHARP PAIN ALONG THE COURSE OF A VEIN

THOSE WHO WENT TO CHINA
Script: Swarn Khandpur
Illustrations: S. K. Parab

AS EARLY AS 65 A.D. TWO BUDDHIST MONKS, DHARMARAKSHA AND KASHYAPA MATANGA, MADE THE PERILOUS JOURNEY TO CHINA CARRYING SACRED BOOKS ON A WHITE HORSE.

THEY WERE WELCOMED BY THE CHINESE EMPEROR, MING TI, WHO BUILT A MONASTERY FOR THEM AND CALLED IT THE WHITE HORSE MONASTERY.

AFTER THAT, SEVERAL HUNDRED BUDDHIST MONKS FROM OUR COUNTRY VISITED CHINA FROM TIME TO TIME. AMONG THEM PARAMARTHA, KUMARAJIVA, BODHIDHARMA AND JIVAGUPTA BECAME VERY FAMOUS.

THESE INDIAN SCHOLARS NOT ONLY CARRIED MANY SANSKRIT MANUSCRIPTS WITH THEM WHICH THEY TRANSLATED INTO CHINESE BUT SOME OF THEM ALSO WROTE ORIGINAL BOOKS IN THE CHINESE LANGUAGE.

MANY INDIAN ARTISANS WERE INVITED FROM THE 'LAND OF THE BUDDHA' BY CHINESE RULERS TO CARVE CAVES, TO PAINT FRESCOES AND TO MAKE BUDDHA'S IMAGES.

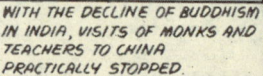

WITH THE DECLINE OF BUDDHISM IN INDIA, VISITS OF MONKS AND TEACHERS TO CHINA PRACTICALLY STOPPED.

IN THE 14TH CENTURY, MUHAMMAD TUGHLUQ SENT IBN BATUTA AS HIS AMBASSADOR TO THE CHINESE COURT.

THEN IN 1924, RABINDRANATH TAGORE VISITED CHINA TO RE-ESTABLISH CULTURAL TIES...

...AND IN 1954, INDIAN AND CHINESE LEADERS EXCHANGED VISITS AND ESTABLISHED DIPLOMATIC TIES.

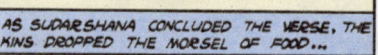

COLOURFUL GIANTS

- Script: Luis Fernandes
- Illustrations: **Ramanand Bhagat**

BIRDWINGS ARE THE GIANTS OF THE BUTTERFLY WORLD. SOME OF THEM HAVE A WINGSPAN OF MORE THAN 300 MM. THE FIRST EUROPEANS TO SEE THESE BUTTERFLIES WERE ASTONISHED AT THE SIZE OF THE INSECTS.

ARE THEY REALLY BUTTERFLIES?

IN 1884, A BUTTERFLY COLLECTOR HEROICALLY SHOT DOWN ONE IN THE SOLOMON ISLANDS AND TOOK IT HOME. THIS GIANT BUTTERFLY (IT BELONGS TO THE SPECIES KNOWN AS QUEEN VICTORIA'S BIRDWING) CAN STILL BE SEEN IN THE COLLECTIONS OF THE BRITISH MUSEUM IN LONDON (SEE INSET).

IN 1908, ANOTHER MAN SHOT DOWN THE LARGEST AND GRANDEST BUTTERFLY OF THEM ALL— QUEEN ALEXANDRA'S BIRDWING.

PICTURE OF SPECIMEN IN BRITISH MUSEUM

THE FEMALE OF QUEEN ALEXANDRA'S BIRDWING HAS A WINGSPAN OF NEARLY 330 MM. IT IS THE LARGEST BUTTERFLY KNOWN. THE MALE IS PUNY IN COMPARISON, HAVING A WING SPAN OF ONLY ABOUT 254 MM. THE FEMALES OF ALL SPECIES OF BIRDWINGS, IN FACT, ARE LARGER THAN THE MALES.
THE FEMALES HOWEVER LACK THE SPECTACULAR MARKINGS THE MALES HAVE ON THEIR WINGS.

BIRDWINGS OCCUR IN SOUTHERN INDIA, SRI LANKA, NORTHERN AUSTRALIA, NEW GUINEA AND THE SOLOMON ISLANDS AND SOME OTHER COUNTRIES IN THE REGION. THEY LIVE ON TOPS OF TREES AND ARE RARELY SEEN. BUT WHEN THEY FLY DOWN THEY ARE EASY TO CATCH AS THEIR FLIGHT IS SLOW.

THE SWALLOWTAIL FAMILY

BIRDWINGS BELONG TO THE SWALLOWTAIL FAMILY OF BUTTERFLIES OF WHICH THERE ARE 600 SPECIES. ONE CHARACTERISTIC OF THIS FAMILY IS THE LONG TAIL ON EACH OF THE HINDWINGS. THE CATERPILLARS OF MANY SPECIES OF SWALLOWTAIL FEED ON POISONOUS CREEPERS. THE POISON TAKEN IN MAKES NOT ONLY THE CATERPILLAR BUT ALSO THE ADULT BUTTERFLY DISTASTEFUL TO BIRDS.

SOME SPECIES OF BIRDWINGS ARE VERY RARE AND FETCH ENORMOUS PRICES. IN 1966 AT AN AUCTION IN PARIS, A VERY RARE BIRDWING "TROIDES ALLOTAI" FROM THE SOLOMON ISLANDS WAS SOLD FOR THE PRINCELY SUM OF £ 1800, ABOUT 20,000 RUPEES.*

* AS PER THE CONVERSION RATE OF THE TIME.

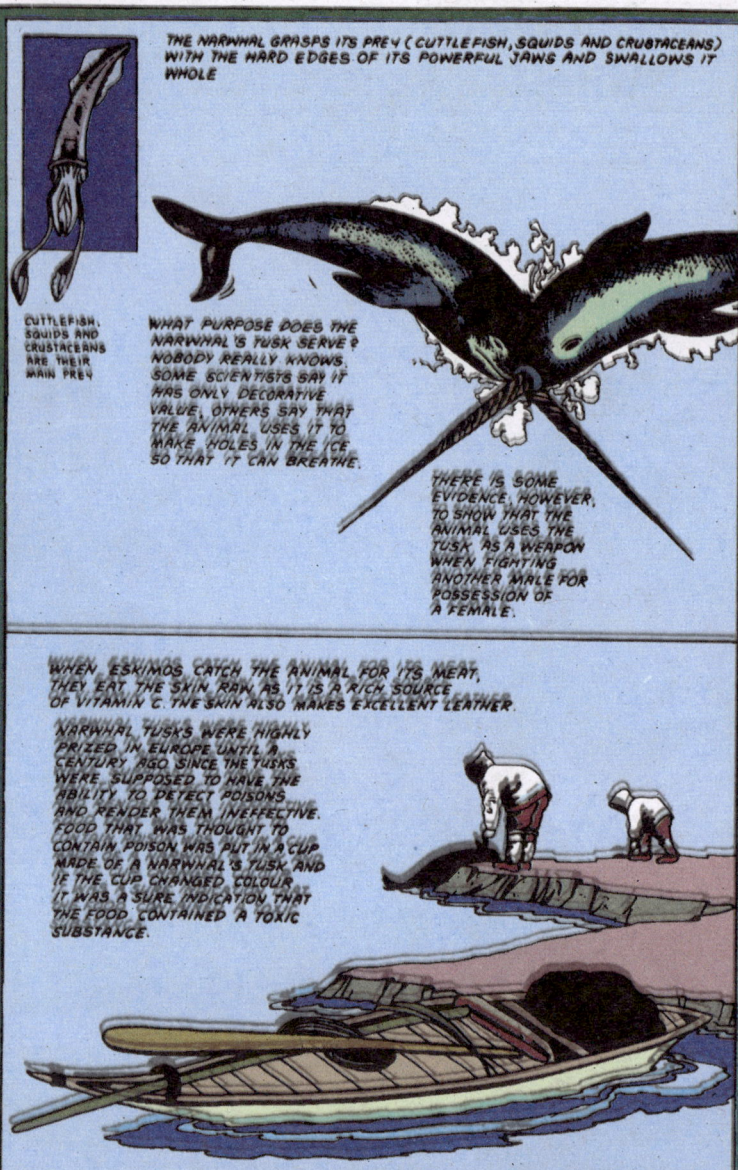

KALIA THE CROW

Based on an idea sent by Master Sushant Bhat
Illustrations: Prasad Iyer

*ANNA MEANS ELDER BROTHER IN KANNADA.

* VILLAGE COURT

SUPER ANIMALS!

FACT FANTASY
Anant Pai • Pradeep Sathe

PASHT, THE EGYPTIAN GODDESS OF FEMINITY AND MATERNITY

CATS, WORSHIPPED IN ANCIENT EGYPT, WERE BURNT ALIVE AND EVEN CRUCIFIED AS WITCHES IN THE MIDDLE AGES BY EUROPEANS!

NAGAPANCHAMI

SERPENTS, CONSIDERED THE SYMBOL OF THE SATAN BY PEOPLE IN THE MIDDLE EAST, EUROPE AND AMERICA, ARE WORSHIPPED IN INDIA AND MANY PARTS OF AFRICA!

MANY PRIMITIVE TRIBES THOUGHT THAT THE INSECT, PRAYING MANTIS, WHICH SITS WITH FOLDED HANDS WAITING FOR ITS PREY, HAD SUPER-HUMAN POWERS AND EVEN ADDRESSED THEIR QUERIES TO THEM.

* BURNING THE WOUND WITH A RED HOT IRON

THE UNREPENTANT MILKMAN

SCRIPT AND ILLUSTRATIONS: P.G. SHARMA.

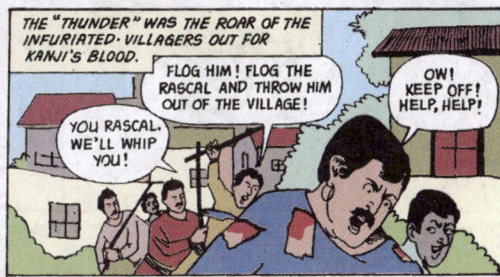

THE TALE OF NESTS

FACT FANTASY
Anant Pai • Pradeep Sathe

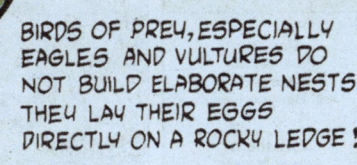

BIRDS OF PREY, ESPECIALLY EAGLES AND VULTURES DO NOT BUILD ELABORATE NESTS. THEY LAY THEIR EGGS DIRECTLY ON A ROCKY LEDGE!

MOST SEA BIRDS LIKE SEAGULLS AND SHORE BIRDS LIKE FLAMINGOES HATCH EGGS IN SHALLOW DEPRESSIONS. MADE ON SHORE BY SCOOPING OUT MUD. SMALL BIRDS, PARTICULARLY THOSE WHOSE YOUNG ONES ARE HATCHED BLIND, NAKED AND HELPLESS, BUILD ELABORATE NESTS, HIGH UP ON TREES.

GORILLAS, COMMONLY FOUND IN AFRICA, ORANGUTANS, THE POWERFUL APES MOSTLY FOUND IN INDONESIA, CHIMPANZEES AND SEVERAL SMALLER APES TOO BUILD NESTS LIKE PLATFORMS IN TREES!

KALIA THE CROW

Script:- Luis Fernandes
Illustrations:- Prasad Iyer

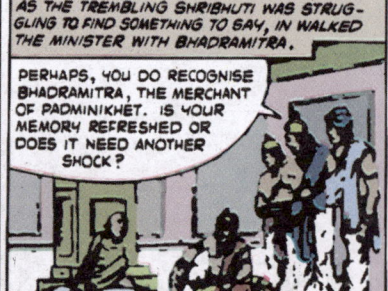

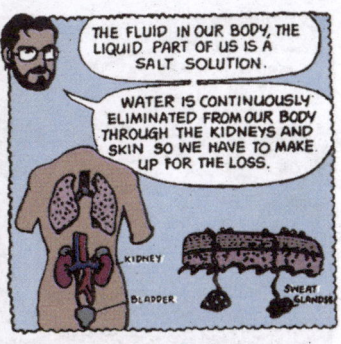

*TRUE TO THE SALT +UNTRUE TO THE SALT

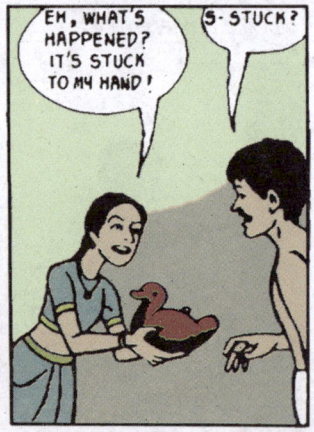

THE AMAZING DOLPHIN

Script: Prasad Iyer
Illustrations: Goutam Sen

ONE OF THE MOST REMARKABLE CREATURES OF THE SEA IS THE DOLPHIN — A CREATURE THAT IS NOW FAST BECOMING A VALUABLE ALLY OF MAN IN HIS QUEST TO CONQUER THE OCEANS.

DOLPHINS ARE MAMMALS MEASURING 2-3 METRES IN LENGTH AND WEIGHING 200-400 KG. LIKE OTHER MAMMALS THEY BREATHE AIR AND WOULD DROWN IF THEY STAYED UNDERWATER FOR TOO LONG — A DOLPHIN CAN REMAIN SUBMERGED FOR PERHAPS ONLY SIX MINUTES AT A TIME.

THEY ARE FAST SWIMMERS AND CAN TOUCH SPEEDS OF 30-40 KM PER HOUR.

THE MOST REMARKABLE ASPECT OF THIS MAMMAL IS ITS ABILITY TO LOCATE OBJECTS BY ECHO-SOUNDING.

THEY SEND OUT HIGH-PITCHED SOUNDS AND CAN LOCATE OBJECTS BY LISTENING TO THE ECHOES.

SCIENTISTS HAVE NOTED THAT EVEN BLINDFOLDED DOLPHINS CAN EASILY MAKE THEIR WAY THROUGH A COMPLEX OBSTACLE COURSE USING ONLY THEIR ABILITY TO LOCATE THINGS WITH THE HELP OF ECHOES.

THE DOLPHIN'S ECHO-SOUNDING SYSTEM IS SO EFFICIENT THAT IT CAN EVEN TELL THE COMPOSITION AND SIZE OF AN OBJECT IN FRONT OF IT. SCIENTISTS CARRIED OUT AN INTERESTING EXPERIMENT TO TEST THIS. A BLINDFOLDED DOLPHIN WAS OFFERED A REAL FISH AND A PLASTIC FISH. EACH TIME THE DOLPHIN CHOSE THE REAL ONE AND IGNORED THE PLASTIC FISH!

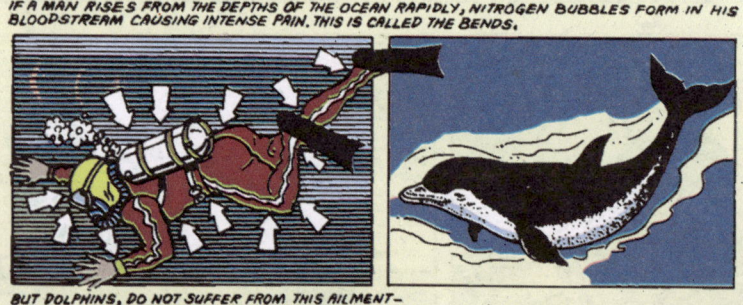

IF A MAN RISES FROM THE DEPTHS OF THE OCEAN RAPIDLY, NITROGEN BUBBLES FORM IN HIS BLOODSTREAM CAUSING INTENSE PAIN. THIS IS CALLED THE BENDS.

BUT DOLPHINS, DO NOT SUFFER FROM THIS AILMENT— A FACT THAT PUZZLED SCIENTISTS FOR QUITE SOME TIME.

BUT THE PUZZLE WAS SOLVED WHEN SCIENTISTS OBSERVED THE UNDERWATER MOVEMENTS OF A TRAINED DOLPHIN NAMED TUFFY.

UNDERWATER CAMERAS REVEALED THAT AT GREAT DEPTHS TUFFY'S CHEST JUST COLLAPSED UNDER THE PRESSURE INDICATING THAT A DOLPHIN'S RIB-CAGE IS FLEXIBLE. THE ELASTIC NATURE OF ITS CHEST AND LUNGS SOMEHOW PREVENTS TOO MUCH NITROGEN FROM GETTING INTO THE BLOOD AND SO A DOLPHIN CAN RISE RAPIDLY FROM GREAT DEPTHS WITHOUT NITROGEN BUBBLES FORMING IN ITS BLOODSTREAM.

THE DOLPHIN CAN BE EASILY TRAINED. THEY HAVE BEEN TRAINED TO TAKE TOOLS TO UNDERWATER DIVERS...

...AND EVEN TO CHASE AWAY SHARKS, INDICATING THE POSSIBILITY THAT DOLPHINS CAN BE USED AS UNDERWATER "WATCHDOGS".

THE DOLPHIN IS VERY FRIENDLY TOWARDS MAN. ATTACKS BY WILD DOLPHINS ON HUMAN BEINGS ARE UNKNOWN.

DOLPHINS ARE VERY INTELLIGENT AND CAN BE TRAINED TO PERFORM A VARIETY OF STUNTS.

THE MERRY COBBLER

Illustrations: Anand Mande

Readers' Choice
Based on a story sent by: Melvin Barboza

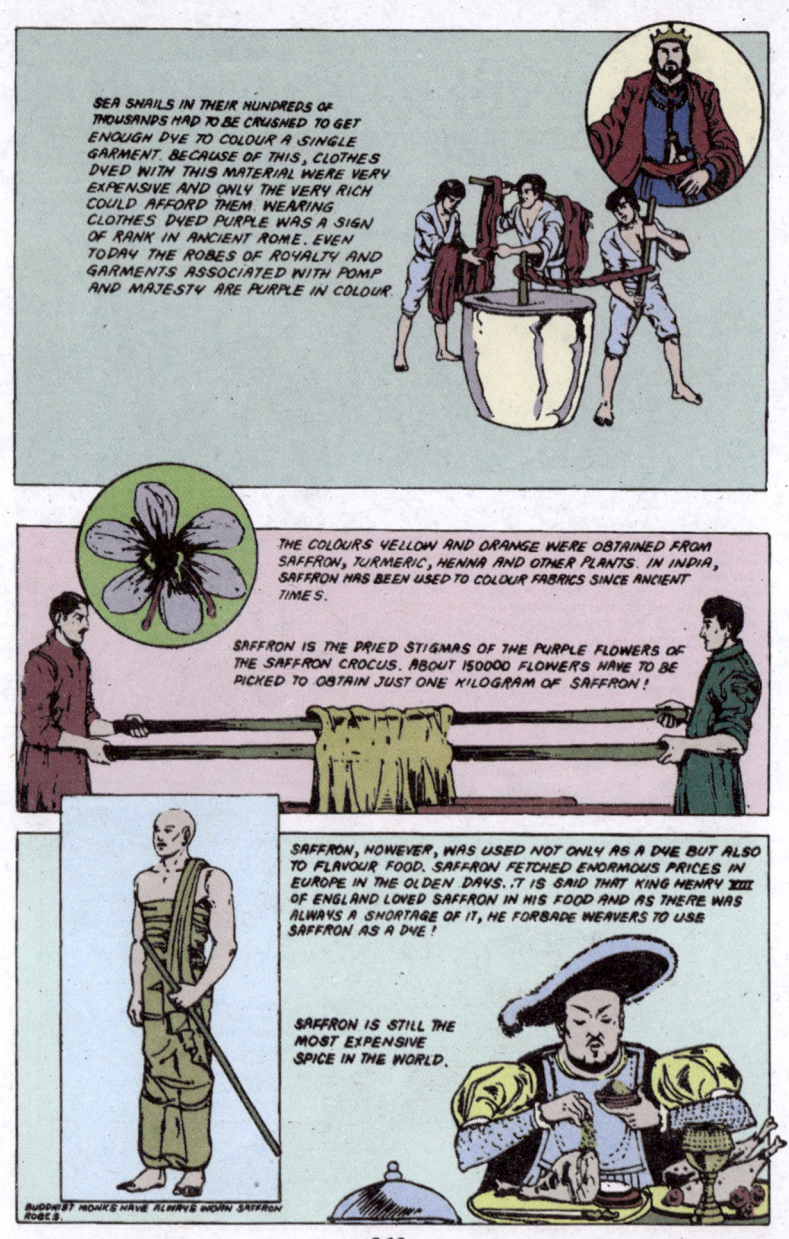

FORMERLY ONE OF THE BRIGHTEST REDS WAS OBTAINED FROM THE COCHINEAL INSECT "DACTYLOPIUS COCCUS" NATIVE TO MEXICO. THE INSECTS WERE KILLED BY DIPPING THEM IN HOT WATER AND THEN THEY WERE DRIED AND CRUSHED TO POWDER. ABOUT 140000 INSECTS WERE REQUIRED TO PRODUCE ONE KILOGRAM OF THE DYE.

PEOPLE ALL OVER THE WORLD WERE RELYING ON THESE FEW NATURAL SUBSTANCES FOR COLOUR UNTIL 1856 WHEN WILLIAM HENRY PERKIN PRODUCED BY ACCIDENT THE COLOUR 'MAUVE' IN HIS LABORATORY AND THUS USHERED IN THE ERA OF SYNTHETIC DYES. BY THE LATE 19TH CENTURY SEVERAL SYNTHETIC DYES HAD BEEN PRODUCED. NOW ABOUT 7,000 OR SO SYNTHETIC DYES ARE AVAILABLE.

A FORTUNATE DISCOVERY

PERKIN DISCOVERED A DYE WHILE TRYING TO PRODUCE QUININE IN THE LABORATORY. DR. GERHARD DOMAGK, ON THE OTHER HAND, WAS STUDYING THE PROPERTIES OF A DYE CALLED PRONTOSIL RED AND DISCOVERED THAT IT KILLED MICROBES. SOON DOCTORS BEGAN TO USE PRONTOSIL IN THE TREATMENT OF VARIOUS DISEASES. IT WAS THE FIRST OF THE DRUGS WHICH CAME TO BE KNOWN AS SULFA DRUGS.

SILVER

Script: Prasad Iyer

Illustrations: Anand Mande

WINNING ONE VICTORY AFTER ANOTHER THE INVINCIBLE ARMY OF ALEXANDER THE GREAT WAS MARCHING THROUGH NORTH-WESTERN INDIA.

IT SEEMED AS THOUGH NO POWER ON EARTH COULD STOP IT.

THEN SUDDENLY A MYSTERIOUS GASTRO-INTESTINAL DISEASE STRUCK THE ARMY. SOLDIERS FELL ILL IN THEIR HUNDREDS. EXHAUSTED AND HOME-SICK THE TROOPS DEMANDED TO RETURN HOME...

...AND ALEXANDER HAD TO YIELD.

BUT IT WAS NOTED THAT THE OFFICERS FELL ILL LESS FREQUENTLY THAN THE COMMON SOLDIERS – A FACT THAT OFTEN PUZZLED ANCIENT HISTORIANS. AND IT WAS ONLY SOME 2000 YEARS LATER THAT SCIENTISTS COULD GIVE AN EXPLANATION. THE OFFICERS OF ALEXANDER'S ARMY DRANK WATER FROM SILVER CUPS UNLIKE THE MEN WHO DRANK FROM TIN CUPS.

SILVER HAS GERMICIDAL PROPERTIES – INDEED A FEW THOUSAND-MILLIONTHS OF A GRAM CAN PURIFY ONE LITRE OF WATER

AND THAT IS WHY ALEXANDER'S OFFICERS REMAINED HALE AND HEARTY WHILE THE MEN BECAME SICK

THIS PURIFYING ACTION OF SILVER WAS KNOWN TO PEOPLE OF OTHER LANDS. THE ANCIENT HISTORIAN HERODOTUS TELLS US HOW THE PERSIAN KING CYRUS, WHEN ON THE MARCH, KEPT HIS WATER IN SACRED SILVER VESSELS

AND ANCIENT INDIAN RELIGIOUS TEXTS DESCRIBE HOW WATER WAS PURIFIED BY IMMERSING WHITE-HOT SILVER IN IT.

BUT IT IS IN COINAGE THAT SILVER FOUND ITS NICHE IN ANCIENT TIMES. IT IS BELIEVED THAT SILVER COINS WERE MADE IN INDIA, PERSIA, EGYPT AND THE COUNTRIES BETWEEN THE SINDHU AND THE NILE SINCE 600 B.C.

SILVER DENARII OF THE ROMAN REPUBLIC C 140 B.C

SILVER DRACHMA OF ATHENS, C 450 B.C

SILVER THALER OF SIGISMUND, ARCHDUKE OF AUSTRIA, 1439-89

SILVER PENNY OF ALFRED THE GREAT, KING OF WESSEX, 871-899

SILVER GROAT OF HENRY V, KING OF ENGLAND 1413-22

THE ROMANS MINTED SILVER COINS IN 269 B.C. 50 YEARS BEFORE GOLD COINS

AND ALL OVER THE WORLD SILVERSMITHS USED THE METAL TO TURN OUT COUNTLESS ORNAMENTS.

SOMETIMES THIS PRECIOUS METAL WAS USED FOR RIDICULOUS PURPOSES. THE ROMAN EMPEROR NERO HAD THOUSANDS OF HIS MULES SHOD WITH SILVER.

IN THE MODERN WORLD TOO SILVER MAINTAINS ITS ROLE AS A JEWELLER'S AND CRAFTSMAN'S METAL.

...BUT IT IS ALSO USED IN INDUSTRY

SILVER BROMIDE AND SILVER CHLORIDE, COMPOUNDS OF SILVER, ARE USED IN PHOTOGRAPHIC FILMS.

WHEN LIGHT FALLS ON A PHOTOGRAPHIC FILM THE SILVER BROMIDE OR SILVER CHLORIDE DISINTEGRATES. SILVER IS PRECIPITATED AND THE IMAGE IS FORMED.

JUMPING JOKER

You will need:

1. 3 playing cards (Ace, King and the Joker)
2. A strip of celo-tape
3. A rubberband cut in the middle

1. Stick one end of the rubberband on the front of one card (say the Ace) 1 to 15 cm from the top with the help of the cello-tape. Stick the other end of the rubberhand on to the back of the other card (the King).

2. Now display the 3 cards to your friends as shown.
3. Keep the Joker in between the 2 cards attached by the rubberband. You will have to push it a little but your friends must not know that you are using force. After pushing in the Joker hold the three cards tightly together.

4. Tell your friends that the Joker will jump out if any one of them holds your wrist. As soon as your friend holds your wrist, loosen your grip and lo! The Joker jumps up!

Idea sent by:
Kishore Chhatwani

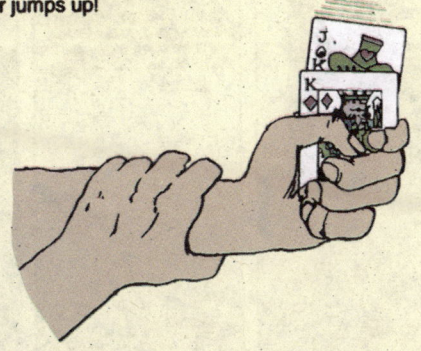

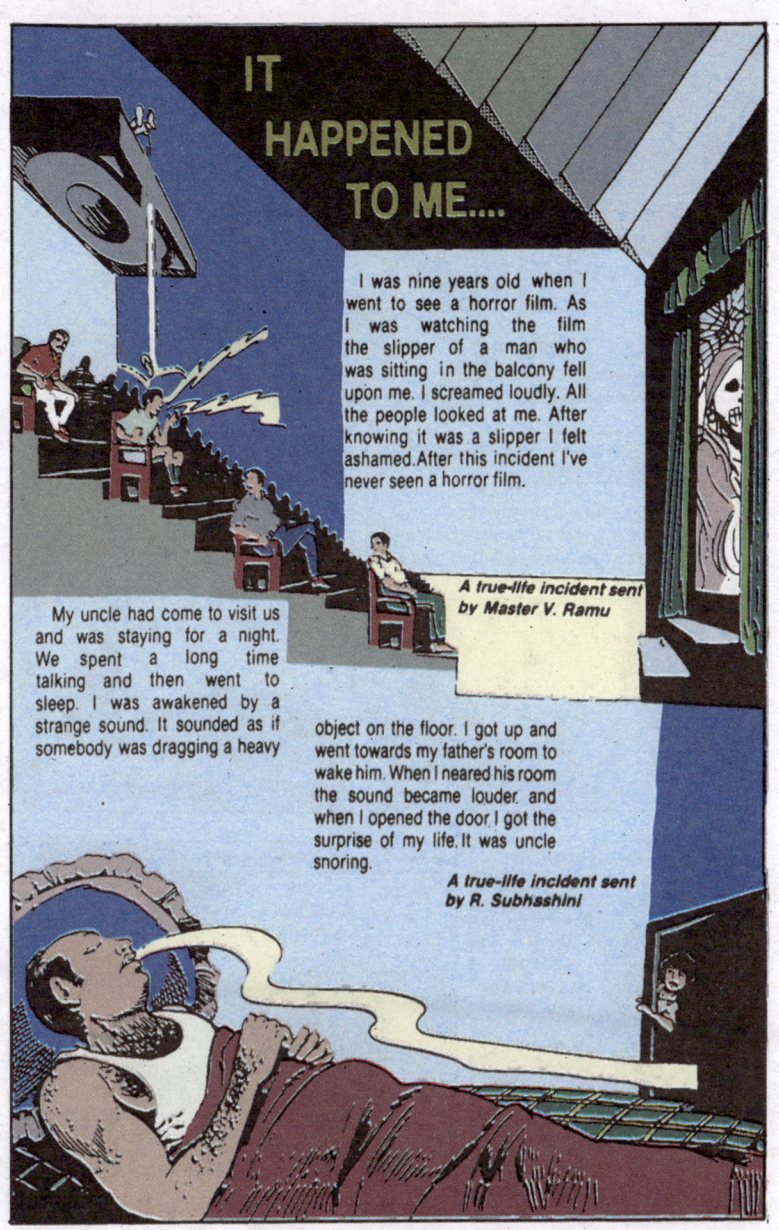

TRAPPING THE SUN!

FACT FANTASY
Anant Pai • Pradeep Sathe

IN 1924, DR. HARRY STEENBOCK DEMONSTRATED THAT BABY RATS TRIPLED THEIR WEIGHTS IN A FEW WEEKS, WHEN THEIR RATION WAS EXPOSED TO THE RAYS OF THE SUN FOR TEN MINUTES!

THE BENEFICIAL EFFECT IS DUE TO VITAMIN D. THIS IS PRODUCED BY EXPOSING MILK OR MILK PRODUCTS TO THE RAYS OF THE SUN, PREFERABLY AROUND SUNRISE AND SUNSET. GRANDMA KNEW HOW TO TRAP THE SUN IN MANY OF HER FOOD PREPARATIONS!

EVEN BY EXPOSING HUMAN SKIN TO SUN'S RAYS IN THE EARLY MORNING VITAMIN D CAN BE "MANUFACTURED" FROM ERGOSTEROLS IN THE SKIN. BUT BEWARE! TOO MUCH OF EXPOSURE TO SUNLIGHT IS NOT GOOD FOR HEALTH!

MARVELS IN STONE

Script : Swarn Khandpur (Halebid, Belur and Somnathpur) Illustrations : S. K. Parab

THE HOYSALAS WHO ROSE TO POWER IN KARNATAKA IN THE 12TH CENTURY A.D., ARE REMEMBERED TODAY FOR THEIR BEAUTIFUL TEMPLES AT HALEBID, BELUR AND SOMNATHPUR.

VERY DISTINCT IN STYLE, THESE TEMPLES ARE BUILT ON RAISED PLATFORMS AND DO NOT HAVE THE TALL GOPURAMS, SO TYPICAL OF SOUTH-INDIAN TEMPLES.

THE NAME "HOYSALA" HAS AN INTERESTING ORIGIN. "HOY, SALA" (MEANING, STRIKE, SALA,) WERE THE WORDS SPOKEN TO SALA, A HUNTER. WHEN A HERMIT WAS THREATENED BY A TIGER SALA KILLED THE TIGER. THE HERMIT BLESSED HIM WITH SOVEREIGNTY FOR SAVING HIS LIFE. SALA LATER FOUNDED A KINGDOM AND HIS HEROIC ACT BECAME THE EMBLEM OF THE DYNASTY.

THE HOYSALA TEMPLES ARE HIGHLY DECORATIVE. THEY HAVE ELABORATE CARVED FRIEZES RUNNING ROUND THEIR WALLS. THE FRIEZE REPRODUCED HERE DEPICTS A SCENE FROM THE PANCHATANTRA STORY OF THE TURTLE WHO FELL OFF THE STICK. THESE HIGHLY CHISELLED FRIEZES ARE INTERSPERSED WITH LARGER FIGURES OF DANCERS, MUSICIANS AND HUNTERS. IN THE KESAVA TEMPLE (SOMNATHPUR) EVEN GANESHA IS SHOWN DANCING.

SUPPORTING THE EAVES OF THE TEMPLES ARE ORNATE FIGURES IN GRACEFUL POSES.

THE INTERIORS OF THESE TEMPLES ARE AS ORNATE AS THEIR EXTERIORS WITH FINELY CARVED PILLARS. AND THIS NANDI, VAHAN* OF SHIVA, SEEMS TO HAVE RECEIVED SPECIAL ATTENTION FROM THE SCULPTOR.

*VEHICLE

IT HAPPENED TO ME....

Once we were off for my cousin's wedding and we boarded two rickshaws. My mother and I drove in the first rickshaw along with the luggage. The rickshaw stopped in the front of the S.T. stand. My mother got down and went in search of the other rickshaw. The luggage from our rickshaw was unloaded in a hurry and neither my mother nor I remembered the suitcase placed in the back compartment of the rickshaw. It contained the gifts for the bridegroom and also my mother's jewellery. The rickshaw went away with the suitcase.

It was only later that we realised that the suitcase had not been unloaded. My father was furious. We had not noted the number of the rickshaw but I remembered the attractive display of stickers on the windscreen. My father and I enquired at the rickshaw drivers' union outside the S.T. stand. I described the radium sticker with the picture of a cobra to the union leader. He instantly recognised the rickshaw. He searched the register and led us to the rickshaw driver's house. Fortunately the rickshaw driver had just returned. He hadn't noticed the suitcase. When we told him about it, he told us that we were lucky that no other passenger had boarded the rickshaw after we had left. My father rewarded him and thanked him as well as the union leader.

Both the rickshaw driver and the union leader praised me for my keen powers of observation.

A true-life incident sent by Adil Fakih

It was the first day in school after the vacations. I was then in the third standard and my sister in the first standard. My mother had asked me to look after my sister in the school. Our English teacher was in the classroom and she was teaching us grammar. I happened to look out of the window and saw my sister, Kalpana, walking out of the gate. Without a second thought I yelled "Kalpana." Then realising what I had done I saw the whole class staring at me. The teacher walked up to me and I thought I would receive a slap. I was about to apologise when she said: "Well, what are you waiting for? Go and get her!"

I could not believe my ears. I ran and brought my sister and kept her with me till the end of class.

A true-life incident sent by S. Meena.

ALL ABOUT SNAKES!

FACT FANTASY
Anant Pai • Pradeep Sathe

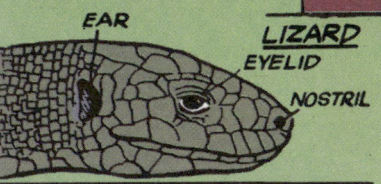

LIZARD — EAR, EYELID, NOSTRIL

SNAKE — NOSTRIL

THAT SNAKES SHED THEIR SKIN SEVERAL TIMES IN A YEAR IS USUALLY KNOWN, BUT NOT MANY KNOW THAT SNAKES HAVE NEITHER EARS, NOR EYELIDS AND CANNOT HEAR.

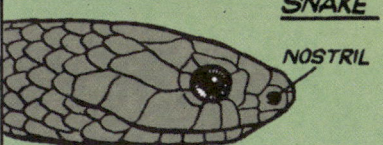

WHEN IT SWAYS TO THE BEEN*, COBRA IS JUST TRYING TO GET INTO A POSITION TO STRIKE AT THE SWAYING THING. IF THE "BEENWALA" KEEPS HIS BEEN STATIONARY, THE SERPENT WILL STRIKE AT IT!

A SNAKE'S HEART CONTINUES TO BEAT FOR MANY HOURS, AFTER YOU CUT OFF ITS HEAD. A SNAKE'S MOUTH IS SUCH THAT IT CAN SWALLOW AN EGG MANY TIMES WIDER THAN IT!

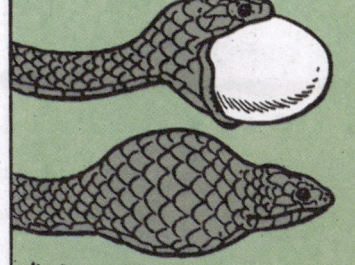

* A FLUTE-TYPE INSTRUMENT USED BY SNAKE-CHARMERS.

TOKEN MONEY

FACT FANTASY
Anant Pai • Pradeep Sathe

PAPER MONEY WAS FIRST TRIED IN 910 A.D. BY THE CHINESE AND WAS VERY MUCH IN USE BY 970 A.D.

THOUGH MUHAMMAD-BIN-TUGHLUQ WAS PERHAPS THE FIRST TO ISSUE COINS OF LEATHER, HE WAS NOT THE ONLY ONE. BANK NOTES, DATED EARLY 19TH CENTURY, PRINTED ON WALRUS AND SEAL HIDE HAVE BEEN FOUND IN RUSSIA. THEY HAD BEEN ISSUED IN ALASKA BY THE RUSSIAN—AMERICAN COMPANY, FORMED AT THE END OF THE 18TH CENTURY.

"THE PAPER IS MONEY?!"

THE WORLD'S EARLIEST BANK NOTES WERE ISSUED IN STOCKHOLM, SWEDEN, IN 1661 A.D.

THE DUMBBELLS
in Aerobatics

Script: Prasad Iyer
Illustrations: Anand Mande

SHARKS

SCRIPT: SHOBHA RAO
ILLUSTRATIONS: AJIT VASAIKAR

THE MAJORITY OF FISHES LIVING IN THE SEA HAVE BONY SKELETONS. THEY ARE CALLED TELEOSTS WHICH MEANS "MADE OF BONE."

SHARKS AND THEIR RELATIVES, RAYS AND SKATES, DO NOT HAVE BONY SKELETONS. THEIR SKELETONS ARE MADE OF CARTILAGE. THEY'RE CALLED CARTILAGINOUS FISH.

SHARKS HAVE SEVERAL SETS OF TEETH ARRANGED IN ROWS ONE BEHIND THE OTHER. EACH SPECIES OF SHARK HAS A PARTICULAR TYPE OF TOOTH.

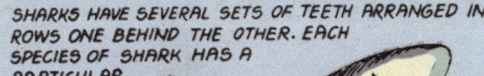

IN CASES OF SHARKBITE, THE SPECIES RESPONSIBLE CAN BE IDENTIFIED BY TOOTHMARKS LEFT ON THE VICTIM. IF A SHARK LOSES A TOOTH IT SOON GROWS A NEW ONE.

JAWS OF WHITE SHARK

THE GREAT WHITE SHARK, FEATURED IN THE FILM "JAWS" IS THE ONE THAT HAS GIVEN ALL SHARKS A BAD NAME. IT WEIGHS AROUND FOUR TONNES BUT IT IS ONE OF THE SWIFTEST SHARKS. IT HAS A TENDENCY TO ATTACK ANYTHING MOVING IN THE WATER WHETHER IT IS A DISCARDED CAR TYRE OR A MAN.

THE FEROCIOUS HAMMERHEAD SHARK IS ANOTHER FISH THAT IS FEARED BY DIVERS.

SOME OTHER SHARKS

SHOWN HERE ARE SOME OF THE LARGER SHARKS. MOST SHARKS, HOWEVER, ARE SMALL, ABOUT A METRE IN LENGTH OR EVEN SMALLER.

PORBEAGLE

BLUE SHARK THE MOST COMMON SPECIES

GREY NURSE SHARK

BASKING SHARK

MATCHBOX FUN

Travelling Eyes

You will need: A matchbox, colours, drawing paper and glue.

 A) Trace this figure on a piece of paper and colour it. Then cut it out and stick it on the matchbox.

 **B)** Cut out two holes for the eyes.

 C) Glue white paper on the "drawer" of the matchbox and paint two big dots so that they coincide with the holes cut out on the outer box.

 Now if you push and pull the "drawer" of the matchbox the "eyes" will travel from side to side.

Sent by: Prashanth Kumar, New Delhi

GET YOUR FORTNIGHTLY DOSE OF ENTERTAINMENT NOW!

- Uninterrupted Tinkle supply
- Amazing D-I-Y projects
- Fresh and exciting stories
- Fascinating trivia
- Fun for the whole family
- Doorstep Delivery

Product	Term	Issues	Cover Price	You Pay	Save	Complimentary Gifts
Tinkle Magazine	1 year	24	₹1200	₹1149	₹51	Two Tinkle folktale collections!
Tinkle Combo	1 year	24+12	₹3120	₹2149	₹971	Four Tinkle folktale collections!

PLEASE ALLOW FOUR TO SIX WEEKS FOR YOUR SUBSCRIPTION TO BEGIN!

OFFER VALID TILL OCTOBER 31ST, 2019

YOUR DETAILS
Full Name: .... Date of Birth: ☐☐ ☐☐ ☐☐☐☐
Address: ....
City: .... State: .... Pin Code: ☐☐☐☐☐☐
Phone/Mobile No.: ☐☐☐ ☐☐☐☐☐☐☐☐☐☐
Email: ....

Parent's Signature

PAYMENT OPTIONS
Cheque/DD: ☐☐☐☐☐☐ drawn in favour of 'ACK MEDIA DIRECT LTD.' on bank
.... for amount .... Dated: ☐☐ / ☐☐ / ☐☐

SEND US YOUR COMPLETED FORM WITH YOUR CHEQUE/DD AT:
ACK Media Direct Ltd, AFL House, 7th Floor, Lok Bharati Complex, Marol-Maroshi Road, Andheri (East), Mumbai 400 059.

MORE WAYS TO SUBSCRIBE: www.amarchitrakatha.com | customerservice@ack-media.com | +91-22-49188881/2

*T &C Apply